⊙ GYPSY GIRL'S BEST SHOES ⊙

GYPSY GIRL'S BEST SHOES

by ANNE ROCKWELL

PARENTS' MAGAZINE PRESS
A DIVISION OF PARENTS' MAGAZINE ENTERPRISES, INC.
NEW YORK

FOR HANNAH AND ELIZABETH

Once there was a little gypsy girl named Maggi. She wandered the wide world over with her gypsy mother and daddy, and one day, they came to a great, big city.

They moved into an empty store with a bright blue front. Maggi's mother told fortunes from her crystal ball, and they all lived behind the curtains, in the back of the store. In the evenings they sang songs about the many places they had been. They were a very happy family.

The store had once been a shoe store, and one day, on the shelf of a closet, Maggi's father found a shoe box. In the box was a pair of brand new, shiny red patent leather shoes that had been forgotten. They were the most beautiful shoes Maggi had ever seen, and they were just her size! They were exactly what a little gypsy girl needed for dancing.

She ran to show them to her mother, who was sitting at the table with a lady wearing a fancy hat. "Oh, they are lovely!" exclaimed her mother. "How lucky you are that they fit so well."

"May I do a dance for you?" asked Maggi.

"Later, little one," whispered her mother. "This lady would like me to tell her fortune. Run outside and play."

So down the street went Maggi, the gypsy girl,

in her brand new, shiny red patent leather shoes.

She stopped at the firehouse near the corner, and asked the firemen, "May I do a beautiful dance for you in my new red shoes?"

But the fire bell was ringing and the men were jumping on the fire engine. "Not now, gypsy girl," said one of the firemen. "We have to hurry to put out a fire. Come back and dance for us later."

The big red fire engine went roaring away, clanging its bell and blowing its siren.

Maggi went on down the street until she came to the bakery. In she went, and she asked the lady behind the counter, "May I do a dance for you in my brand new shoes?"

"Oh, not now," said the lady. "We're much too busy baking wedding cakes and birthday cakes to stop and watch you. But you may have a cookie if you like."

Maggi said thank you and chose a dark chocolate one.

By the time she reached the corner, Maggi had finished her cookie. Just as she got there she saw a group of men going down a manhole in the middle of the street. "Hello!" she called over to them. "Would you like to see me do a dance for you in my beautiful new shoes?"

"We're sorry, gypsy girl," said one of the men, "but we have to fix a lot of wires down in this hole. We don't have time for a dancing show right now." And with that they all disappeared under the street.

Maggi turned around. There was a pet store, filled with dogs and cats, hamsters, birds, and fish. She thought about going in and doing her dance there, but the dogs were barking, the birds were twittering, and a large green parrot was screeching inside a large brass cage. Only the fish were silent as they darted about in their bubbling tanks of water.

"Nobody would hear my jingly tambourine with all that noise," said Maggi to herself, and she walked on past the pet store.

Maggi was feeling a little sad now, so she went into a flower shop just to sniff all the good smells. "May I do a dance for you in my beautiful new red shoes?" she asked the lady in a small voice.

"My, they *are* pretty shoes," the lady said. "But Mrs. Fielding-Jones is having a party tonight, and I must arrange all these flowers for her. I'm afraid I haven't time to stop." Then she smiled. "Here is a red rose for you to match your shoes."

"Thank you," said Maggi, and out she went into the street again.

Up one block and down the other she went,

looking for someone who would watch her dance,

but everybody was too busy.

At last she came to the end of the street, and there was the park, all cool and green. Pigeons cooed, squirrels chattered, and a soft breeze fluttered the leaves on the trees. Maggi had never been this far from home in the store, and she had never seen the park. She decided to go in.

People were sleeping in the sun on the grass, old ladies were feeding pigeons, and a row of nursemaids in white dresses sat together on a bench knitting.

"Excuse me," said Maggi. "I have brand new shiny red patent leather shoes, and a red, red rose and a tambourine. I would like to do a dance for you. I'm sure you would like it very much."

"Oh, my goodness no!" cried one of the nursemaids. "Your dancing feet and jangling tambourine would surely wake our babies, and then they would cry."

"Run along, little girl," said another. "We don't want any noise here!"

Maggi turned and walked quietly away. She found an empty bench, far away from anybody, and sat down. She wiggled her toes inside her new shoes, and watched the sun make shiny spots on them. Then she softly jingle-jangled her tambourine. A little squirrel, running past with a peanut, stopped and looked at her.

As Maggi spied him her face brightened. "Maybe, little squirrel," she said, "*you* would like to see my dance." She hopped off the bench, and then, with only a squirrel to watch, she lifted her tambourine, tapped her shiny shoes, twirled her red, red rose, and started to dance.

And she danced. . . .

And danced. . . .

And danced. . . .   And danced. . . .

And finally, with one last spin and a rattle of her jingly tambourine, she stopped.

But what was this she heard? Clapping hands and laughter, and a voice that said, "What a lovely dance! Thank you! Thank you!"

Maggi turned around, and there stood a lady with a smiling, friendly face, and ten little children behind her.

"What a lovely dance!" she said again.

"And so mysterious!" said a little girl.

"And fast!" said one of the boys.

"I wish I knew how to dance like that," said another child.

"Please, please, little girl, dance for us again!" they all cried.

And so Maggi, the gypsy girl, did her dance again, while her brand new, shiny red patent leather shoes sparkled in the sunlight.

Then all the children tumbled and laughed, and
ran around and around in the grass . . . . . .

and picked dandelions together.

At last it was time for everyone to go, but before Maggi left, the lady asked her name and where she lived. "I will speak to your mother," she said. "Perhaps you can come to our school. Then you can dance for us often."

With a wave of her hand to her new friends, Maggi ran out of the park . . .

And she skipped and danced all the way home to

the blue-front store in her brand new, shiny red

patent leather shoes.

THE END